Bear of Trees

Author Ketevan Alexander

Edited by Kevin Anderson & Associates

Illustrated by Irina Tsintsadze

In the Eastern Woods, at the foot of the Bear Mountains, lived a young bear named Betrees. Her shiny fur was as black as a moonless night save for one white, heart-shaped spot on her forehead. It is said that Betrees' mother was a black bear who made a journey to the northern lands. There she fell in love with a polar bear — a great love that resulted in a beautiful black cub with a white, heart-shaped spot on her forehead. But the arctic cold was too much for the tiny cub, so her mother brought her back to the warm and mild Eastern Woods. Betrees was soon fascinated by the trees and quickly learned to climb them. The great trunks and branches became the cub's playground, and so her mother named her Bear of Trees — Betrees for short.

Soon the cub grew into a strong and beautiful bear. Mother taught Betrees how to protect herself and to fish for fat salmon in the mountain creek. When she turned two, Betrees was ready to move into a den of her own. She was happy and content in her cozy home on a hill in the Eastern Woods, close to the freshwater creek.

Betrees loved the woods with all her heart, and was very grateful for everything she had. The only thing missing from her life was love. A true love. She had several admirers in the Eastern Woods, but none of them were even close to what her heart desired.

Hoping for some wise advice, Betrees visited a well-known fortuneteller and oracle—the old lady owl. The oracle was very clever, but she always talked in riddles. Sometimes it was very hard to understand her. She told Betrees that her true love lived in the Northern Woods, but that she would meet him in the Western Woods after many, many moons. She didn't say exactly how many. Betrees, believing what the oracle told her, made a long trip up to the north. But, alas, she didn't meet anyone who could capture her tender and loving heart. She returned to her home very disappointed. The only hope for her now was the Western Woods, but first she needed a good rest.

It was already the end of autumn and as her mother had taught her, Betrees prepared her home for the long sleep.

When at long last Betrees opened her eyes, bright sunlight filled her den. "Oh my goodness!" she exclaimed. "I must have overslept!"

And she certainly had, for all the rich scents of spring in full bloom filled the air.

Betrees slipped down from her fluffy-puffy bed, shook her fur from head to claws and examined her reflection in the looking glass. She had grown thin during the long winter sleep, and it was time for her to find food. She brushed her coat until it was soft and glossy, put on a nice dress and stepped outside.

"Hello, neighbor. I have not seen you in a long time, where have you been?" came a chirpy voice. Betrees looked up and saw her neighbor, the mischievous squirrel, sitting on the tree branch and wiggling his tail.

"Hello Squirrel! I am very well, thank you. I traveled up to the Northern Woods, then came home for my long winter sleep," Betrees responded.

"Ah, that explains it. It's been so many months since I've seen you, I thought you might have found a new den. Did you like up there, in the north?"

"I did, but I missed my home very much and I am glad I am back."

"You're looking rather lean," Squirrel remarked, for he was very outspoken.

"That happens during the long sleep. Do I look sickly?" Betrees asked, concerned.

"You look as usual to me—hairy and beary. That white heart on your forehead just drives me nuts. If you were a squirrel, I would marry you in a heartbeat."

Betrees giggled and the tip of her nose blushed pink, but Squirrel didn't notice that.

"Well you must be very hungry," continued Squirrel. "I can offer you some nuts, but you probably will need something much more nutritious.

But when you are looking for food please don't go toward the Western Woods. There are humans there now, building themselves a village. During your winter sleep, they built a broad flat road, and now the Metallic River is flowing straight through the center of the woods."

"The Metallic River! What is that?" Betrees asked. It did not sound like something nice.

"Cars," came a low, soft voice from the grass. It was Rabbit, who had hopped over to greet Betrees. "They are vessels of shiny metal that humans use to migrate, instead of using their legs. They flow over the road like waves, and at night they glow like the moon. Then their road looks like a river of moving fire. It is most dangerous."

"Dangerous?" asked a bewildered Betrees.

"Indeed. You must never try to cross the Metallic River. It kills," Rabbit warned. "They say several deer tried, and they were never seen again."

"That is terrible!" Betrees exclaimed, her heart sinking. And how would she ever find her love in the Western Woods if she could not safely travel there?

"But where did you learn of this Metallic River?" continued Betrees, hoping it might all be just Eastern Woods gossip.

"That black bear—the very smart one. He told us all about it last week. He's been here a few times now. I think he was hoping to see you," said Squirrel with a mischievous smile, wiggling his tail even more vigorously.

Betrees blushed again. She knew who the smart black bear was—his name was Kobo, and he was one of her many admirers. He was a bear rights activist and knew a lot about humans. Two years ago Kobo gave some speeches in the Eastern Woods and Betrees had been to one of them.

She remembered how amazed she was by the notion that humans were able to fly like a birds.

"Well," said Betrees, "I suppose it must be true, for Kobo knows a great deal about the ways of humans. Thank you for letting me know he was here, and for warning me about the Metallic River."

"Anytime," Squirrel responded, and Rabbit gave a friendly nod.

Betrees waved goodbye to Squirrel and Rabbit and hurried down to the creek in anticipation of filling her empty belly. Betrees knew this place as well as she knew her own four paws. She grew up here and loved everything about it—the tall chestnut and oak trees, the small streams that flowed down the hill after a long rain—and most of all the clear rushing waters of the creek, brimming over with fat silver fish. There were trout, and catfish, and pink crabs. And what a pleasure it was to take a dip in the crystal clear water on a hot summer day. Happy memories of her time as a cub lifted Betrees' spirits and she began to sing. Bears have many wonderful abilities but singing is not one of them. Her full-throated song woke a mother crow in a nearby pine tree from her morning nap. The crow glared down at Betrees.

"Carrrr, carrrr…," Crow scolded. "Be quiet please! You sound terrible and you are scaring my chicks."

Betrees stopped singing, looked up, and chuckled.

"I sound terrible? Have you ever heard the sound of your own voice, Lady Crow?"

"Indeed I have, and there isn't a thing wrong with it. But your voice is awful, and if you'd any sense you wouldn't sing at all," Crow declared.

"Carr! Carr! Awful!" the crow chicks repeated boldly, craning their necks to peer over the nest. They had never seen a bear before, and while they pushed at each other to get a better view, one chick tumbled out of the nest and landed right on Betrees' shoulder. Mama Crow panicked and begun to fly up and down, cawing in alarm. Betrees carefully climbed up to the tree and gently dropped the chick back into its nest. The other chicks flapped and squawked with excitement at the close-up view of the bear.

"Bravo," they applauded Betrees, clapping their tiny wings. She returned a kind smile to the funny, featherless creatures before climbing back down the tree. Then she looked up at the mother crow who was still cawing.

"Hush now, Lady Crow," shushed Betrees. "You are scaring your own chicks. They are all safe now."

"Now I understand why you have that white heart on your forehead, Bear. You have a very kind heart. Thank you," said Crow as she covered her chicks with her wings to quiet them.

"Anytime," Betrees returned.

Betrees began to walk away, taking one last look over her shoulder at the crows. She lost her footing and fell, rolling down to the hill. The hysterical, loud laughter of the crow family followed her all the way down. She tried to grab hold of a raspberry bush to stop her tumble, but failed. She rolled all the way into the middle of the creek, where the whirlpool was. A tall fountain of water erupted

around her, sparkling dozens of rainbows into the
air.

"Oops!" said Betrees splashing around in the water. "The water feels good though. Never mind the crows. I can't teach them manners anyway."

Betrees washed her body and face and rinsed her mouth. The cool water felt wonderful, but her rumbling stomach gently reminded her why she was here. She stood very still and stared into the water, watching and waiting for fish. After successfully catching three large trout and devouring them, Betrees felt as though she were in seventh heaven. Still in the water, she thanked Mother Earth for nourishing her and for letting her awaken from her long winter slumber into this beautiful, green world. She certainly had more thanks to give, but a husky, loud voice interrupted her prayers.

"Bless my soul, look what we have here! Hello, princess. I am Gojoon, the strongest bear you will ever see. As luck would have it, I happen to be looking for a bride."

A strange bear was standing on the right bank of the creek and looking at Betrees with beady eyes.

"Please go away. I don't know you. I don't want to know you, and I am certainly not your bride."

"Choose your words carefully, girl. You are talking to Gojoon, the strongest bear in the Eastern Woods. I recommend you be obedient!'

Betrees had no patience for bossy males like this one and she growled at him.

"Get lost. I obey no one. I am a free-spirited bear, and I will fight for my freedom of choice if I have to."

"It will be my pleasure to challenge you and conquer you!" Gojoon said with a sly smile and shook his shoulders, as he usually did in front of a lady bears. It was his way of showing his strength and superiority. Determined to chase away the rude intruder, Betrees rose up from the water and charged towards the bank where the stranger was standing. It was a small, sandy beach, surrounded by dense bushes—certainly not the best place to fight a much bigger bear. But at that moment, Betrees didn't care.

In a heartbeat she was standing in front of Gojoon, scratching the sand with her claws in a menacing way. Gojoon was taken aback by Betrees' bravery and retreated slightly.

"You don't need to fight him. I will gladly do it for you if you let me," came a voice from the bushes on her left. Surprised, Betrees looked over and saw a young, very handsome brown bear approaching, surprising Gojoon as well. She didn't know what to say or how to react. As the strange bear approached, Betrees was filled with very sweet feeling, one she never experienced before. She felt her heart melting and dripping down to her claws. How little she knew. It was a love at first sight.

"Hey kid, mind your own business will you? I really don't want to hurt you," Gojoon warned the stranger.

"Go away and leave the young lady alone. You've heard her. She doesn't want you," the handsome stranger replied. He then slowly positioned himself in front of Betrees and signaled for her to move aside.

"She is mine. Period," declared Gojoon with irritation. "Go away or I will kill you. You don't belong here. You are a brown bear. Go back to your north."

"Black and brown don't matter. We are all bears and the woods are our home. I can live anywhere I want. You are old enough to know better."

"You are talking about my age now, you little worm? I will teach you a lesson," growled Gojoon angrily.

The young stranger didn't respond. Instead, he charged. He was well-built and strong and fast. Gojoon was no match for him, and ended up on his knees, begging for his life.

"Go in peace," said the young bear, "and never ever cross my path again. I will kill you if you do."

Gojoon slowly walked backwards, his head hanging down and disappeared into the bushes. The handsome stranger turned to Betrees.

"May I walk you home, young lady?"

Betrees, impressed by his fighting abilities and charmed by his looks responded, "Yes, thank you."

The bears sat on the sand for a while to catch up their breath. The brave brown bear introduced himself as Ben.

"Ben?" repeated Betrees. "It is a lovely name but not common for bears. Where did it come from?"

"It is a long story," said Ben.

"I would love to hear it," Betrees said. She smiled and sat comfortably in front of him.

"It was five years ago," said Ben, "I was a cub of just a few months when my mother first took me fishing down the Snowy River. We were very hungry after the long winter sleep, and the walk to the river exhausted us. Before reaching the fishing grounds, we stopped at the meadow to rest. That night, a huge and horrible male bear attacked us. My mother fought fiercely to protect me, but the attacker was much bigger and stronger and he wounded her badly. I watched from my hiding place, but I couldn't do anything to help her. I was too small. She fell on the ground and did not move at all. Then the grizzly came after me, dragging me out of my shelter. I was sure that I was going to die, but unexpectedly some humans showed up."

"What did they do?" asked Betrees, excitedly.

"They shot him with some darts, which I think had some sleeping potion on them. Grizzly fell, and couldn't get up. My mother was very badly wounded. The man and woman tried very hard to save her life, but there was nothing they could do. My wounds were not as bad. The woman tended them, caressed me and said something in her human language, which of course I didn't understand. But I knew deep inside my heart that she was assuring me everything was going to be okay. She bandaged my wounds, gently picked me up and carried me to their car."

"Car?" Betrees interrupted. "That is a thing the humans migrate in, right?"

"Correct!" responded Ben. "They can migrate very fast and very far in their cars. The humans took me to their village, fed me, and took very good care of me. I even played with their children."

"You played with human cubs?" asked a bewildered Betrees.

"Yes, I did! I had a great fun with them. They named me Benjamin Bear, but called me Ben. I stayed with them until I turned two years old. Then they took me to the woods and set me free. Tears appeared in their eyes when they say goodbye to me. I will always remember their kindness and I do miss them sometimes. But I guess bears were not meant to live with humans. So here I am, in the Eastern Woods and looking for love. Tell me, did I come to the right place?"

Hearing this, Betrees blushed and this time her white heart spot turned to a lovely pink color. Ben found it very attractive.

"I think you did," Betrees responded shyly, "As I am looking for love too."

Ben couldn't have hoped for a better response.

"What is your name?" he asked. "And where did this beautiful white spot came from? I never saw anything like this before."

"My father was a polar bear," Betrees explained with a smile. "I inherited this white spot from him."

"Great inheritance," Ben winked at her.

They slowly walked up to the hill towards Betrees' home. Before getting Betrees safely inside her den, Ben climbed up on a tree and retrieved a large piece of honeycomb. Apparently, he was not only a charmer of lady bears, but of bees as well. They allowed him take a honeycomb from their hive without putting up a fight. Betrees accepted the gift with thanks, and rewarded Ben with a small kiss.

Before saying goodbye, Betrees and Ben agreed
to see each other in two moons. They both were very
happy.

Time could not go by fast enough for Betrees, but she patiently waited for Ben's return. She continued fishing, digging for edible roots and gathering nutritious mushrooms. Gaining weight was very important to her in order to be healthy and beautiful.

Two moons passed, then a third, but Ben did not come back. Betrees, knowing that he was an honest and gentlemanly bear, began to worry.

Maybe he was hurt, she thought, *or maybe Gojoon fought him.* Hundreds of other 'maybes' buzzed in her mind, making her life miserable. After many sleepless nights, Betrees decided to look for him. He certainly was not in the Eastern Woods, as she had already combed every inch of the territory. Betrees didn't know what to do. It was possible that Ben had changed his mind and found a new love. That was a devastating thought and it made her cry terribly. The squirrel family and the rabbit family and even the deer family came over to console her, but she couldn't stop crying. Then the squirrel, who knew everything about everybody in the Eastern Woods, made a suggestion.

"Tonight is a full moon," he said. "Why don't you go and ask the oracle owl for advice? She might be able to help you."

Beetrees liked the idea. She thanked the neighbors for their support and set out to visit the oracle at the very edge of the Eastern Woods. She walked into the night. The full moon shone on her path and helped her to find the way.

The old lady owl was napping on the tree branch after a rather filling supper when Betrees approached her. She looked up at sleeping owl and chuckled. The owl woke up immediately and looked down at Betrees with her huge eyes. "Hut! Hut! Why are you here?" she asked. "What troubles you, young bear?"

"I am looking for a brown bear named Ben, who I love very much. He gave me his promise he would return to me three moons ago, but he did not. Can you please help me to find him?" asked Betrees, her heart pounding heavily.

The owl looked up at the moon, and looked down at Betrees and looked up at the moon again.

"Oh, great and magical moon," she whispered, "we humbly ask you to tell us where Ben is. Oh, moon, tell us!"

For several long minutes the owl did not take her eyes from the moon and Betrees didn't draw a breath.

"He is in the Western Woods," said the owl finally, and Betrees breathed in relief. "He loves you very much, so never doubt his love! But he is in trouble now and needs your help. You must cross the Metallic River to find him."

Betrees' heart sank when she heard that Ben was in trouble. She was ready to go to the end of the world to find him, but crossing the Metallic River sounded almost impossible.

"Cross the Metallic River? But it kills, doesn't it?" she asked.

"It can, but you are clever enough to find a way. Go while it is dark. At night the Metallic River becomes fiery, but it is never whole. There will be some dark gaps in it. You need somehow to skip between those gaps."

"Thank you for your advice oracle," Betrees said, "And I promise I will try my best."

"Moon bless you my child. Go, save your loved one," the old owl encouraged her. "I must watch over my great-grand owlets tonight and can't go with you, but I am very sure you will find a way."

With a heavy heart Betrees followed the owl's directions and soon came face to face to the infamous Metallic River. It was the widest river she had ever seen. Scattered lights were flowing in both directions. Betrees noticed some dark spaces in the flow. She observed the river for a couple of minutes and studied its patterns. The oracle was right. There were gaps between lights from both sides and it should be possible to skip between them. Betrees carefully approached the road, looked up at the bright moon and whispered a prayer, "Magical Moon, please help me to find my way across." As though the sky heard her prayers, two shooting stars zoomed and fizzled past the face of the moon. She took that as a good omen.

Betrees waited patiently for the dark gap, and when it came close she leaped through it. Between the two streams was a small fence and Betrees stopped there for a while.

She waited for another gap in the opposite stream and tried to skip through it when it came close. Suddenly a bright light came around the curve and blinded her. Betrees was scared, but she didn't stop moving. She heard some screeching sounds, but ignored them and ran as fast as she could. She made to the other side safely, and only then did she look back. To her great surprise, the Metallic River was standing still. She got an impression that the flow had stopped just for her. Was it possible that The Metallic River let her pass deliberately? Betrees didn't have an answer but she breathed out a very emotional thanks.

She ran up the hill and stopped at the top for a few minutes. Under the moonshine the sight of totally unfamiliar Western Woods unfolded before her eyes. They covered a huge territory. Betrees remembered what she had been told—there were humans in these woods, and danger might lurk anywhere under the heavy forest canopy. But Betrees

lifted her snout bravely. Her love was strong and her spirits high. She didn't give it a second thought and before the dawn painted the sky red, she had thoroughly combed the woods. She called Ben's name in a very low voice, but there was no answer. Finally, exhausted Betrees found a cluster of dense bushes and curled up underneath them. She dozed. She didn't know how long she slept, but when she woke up the sun was already high in the sky. Suddenly she heard noises and an unfamiliar smell tingled through her nostrils. She went still, filled with alarm. *DANGER!* she thought. Betrees carefully pushed the bush branches apart and looked through them. She saw three two-legged creatures walking on the path. Betrees knew that they were humans. To Betrees' dismay, they noticed her too and froze in their tracks.

"Oh, my heavens," said one loudly, "is that a bear?"

"She has a white heart on her forehead, I never saw anything like it," said another in a very excited voice.

"We need to take a picture of her! Get the cameras, fast! Don't scare her!" said the third human.

Betrees didn't understand the human language, but she knew somehow that they were talking about her. Her mother had always taught her that a strong offence was the best defense. The time to use the advice was now. Betrees lumbered out of the bushes, rose on her back legs and growled. The humans had cameras already aimed at her. A series of flashes and clicks followed and Betrees panicked.

Are those small devices weapons? she wondered. *Are they shooting at me?* She abruptly turned around and took off through the dense woods, breaking the tree branches and the Olympic sprinting record at the same time. After all, she was a strong and fast bear. She had no idea how long or far she ran. Out of breath and exhausted, she halted in a grove of raspberry bushes. Frightened and confused, she tried to catch her breath. Betrees lifted her snout and cried out in desperation. "Ben! Where on Earth are you?"

And then a miracle happened. She heard Ben's voice.

"Over here, Betrees," he called.

Betrees rushed towards the voice and found Ben clinging to a tree branch that was hanging right over the edge of a cliff.

"Hang on!" she shouted. "I'm coming to get you!"

Betrees stepped on a stronger branch of the same tree and pushed it down toward Ben with her hind leg. Ben reached the branch with one paw, clung onto it and slowly pulled himself up. He landed on a solid ground and Betrees' grasp at the same time.

The bears hugged.

"I will never let you go," said Betrees.

"I must have known that," Ben responded. "Because something told me if I hung on long enough, you would save me."

The bears sat next to each other on the grass and hugged again. "But what happened to you, Ben?" asked Betrees

"That old blockhead Gojoon attacked me again. This time he brought two other bears with him. I won, but I barely survived. I had to hide here, in the Western Woods to let my wounds heal. Last night I accidently slipped down from the cliff. Fortunately, I managed to dig my claws into that branch, but I was unable to pull myself up. You came just in time. You saved me!"

"You won a fight with three bears?" asked Betrees, amazed. "You really are my hero!"

Ben responded with a wide grin.

The bears stayed at the raspberry grove until evening. They both needed some time to rest.

Betrees offered to take Ben to her den so she could tend his wounds. She also told him about her encounter with the humans and about the flashing weapons they aimed at her. Ben laughed. He explained to Betrees that humans were shooting at her not with weapons, but with things called cameras. Than he agreed to go to her home and leave the Western Woods as soon as possible.

"We need to cross the Metallic River back. I did it on my way here," said Betrees

Ben looked very surprised. "You really crossed it?"

"Didn't you?" Betrees returned the question.

"First of all, you are the bravest girl bear I have seen in my whole life," Ben told her with admiration. "Second, there is a way to get in and out of the Western Woods without crossing the Metallic River. Humans built a bridge on the creek. We can swim underneath the bridge to the other side."

"I wish I had known that," sighed Betrees. "I was terrified when I crossed the Metallic River."

"I am so sorry you had to go through all that my love. I will never forget it," said Ben, giving her a hearty hug.

"You are more than worth the effort!" Betrees reassured him.

They left the raspberry grove and came down to the creek from the west side. Ben was right, it was possible to swim to the other side without encountering the cars. Before crossing the creek, Betrees saw some lights coming from the bushes at the bank and froze. The bears looked at each other, sniffed the air to detect a possible danger, and carefully approached the light. Betrees saw a large red metallic object, with its wide nose dipping into the creek. She had no idea that they had just found a broken car.

"This looks like a piece of the Metallic River. How did it get here?" she asked Ben.

"I don't know. Let's take a closer look," Ben
suggested.

The bears carefully approached the car and looked inside. A little girl of about six years of age was sitting in the front seat, very still and pale. An older man sitting in front of the steering wheel was also strangely still.

"Are they dead? Does the Metallic River really kill?" asked Betrees breathlessly.

"I don't smell death. I think they are still alive, but we need to get them to other humans as soon as possible. Otherwise, they will die here," Ben told her.

Betrees did not feel comfortable with this idea.

"Are you sure you want to do that? It is not dangerous to get so close to humans?"

"It can be. But I owe them my life, Betrees. It was humans who once saved me, remember?"

Betrees smiled at him and nodded.

"Okay," she agreed. "But those shiny things look very heavy. How can we carry them?"

"We will not carry those. We will carry the girl and the man. The village is not too far from here," Ben replied.

The bears opened the doors of the car and cautiously pulled out the girl and the man, one at a time. Betrees helped Ben to put the man on his back. Then she picked up the girl and gently held her to her chest. She ran on three legs holding the girl with a front paw. Ben ran behind her carrying the man on his back.

It was already dark as they neared the village. From a distance, the whole village looked like a small piece of a starry sky just brought down to the earth. Many bright lights, twinkling like stars, were hurting Betrees' eyes, and she found herself completely amazed by the sight.

'"How do the humans do that?" she asked Ben.

"Do what?" Ben responded.

"Bring the stars down to the Earth."

"Humans are very clever, Betrees. But they do some stupid things too."

"Like what?" she asked curiously.

"Sometimes they finish a meal without eating all of their food. They put what is left in the garbage," said Ben.

Put food in the garbage? Why would anyone do such a thing? Betrees wondered. The thought reminded Betrees how hungry she was.

One house on the outskirts of the village looked more secluded than others, and the bears decided to bring the girl and the man to its door.

Before approaching the house, Ben sniffed the air.

"Why are you sniffing Ben?" asked Betrees.

"I want to be sure there are no dogs in that house. Barking could ruin our whole plan," Ben responded.

Betrees had heard about dogs. She hoped there weren't any inside this house.

The bears quietly approached the door. Betrees very gently and carefully put the girl down on the front porch. As the girl touched the ground, her eyes opened. A faint smile flashed across her pale face when she looked at Betrees.

"Bear! Who painted a white heart on your forehead? It is very beautiful," the girl murmured. Then she closed her eyes and drifted off again.

Betrees had no idea what the girl's words meant. Ben gently put the man down next to the girl, and rang the doorbell. Both bears then scampered into the bushes and hid. They watched as the people in the house opened the front door and came out, amazed to discover the girl and the man. The humans called for help.

"We can go home now," said Ben.

Betrees, still feeling the little girl's heartbeat on her chest, asked, "Will they survive, Ben?"

"Let's hope so," he responded, giving Betrees a hearty hug.

*****

The villagers were all excited by the news that some Good Samaritans had saved a little girl and her father from a car accident. Everybody wanted to meet them, thank them and shake their hands, but the Good Samaritans had simply vanished into the thin air. The village was abuzz with rumors about their identity. Some even said extraterrestrials were to thank for the miracle.

A few days later, the little girl awoke from her coma. She told everyone in the village who it was that had saved her and her father. Not a human. Certainly not an alien. No, it was a black bear, she declared, with a painted white heart on her forehead, who had saved her life. Nobody believed the girl until some local hikers shared the photos they had taken of Betrees. That changed everything. The villagers began to believe what had once seemed impossible—that bears have tender hearts and are willing to save human lives. The news soon made it to the national media and Betrees' photo appeared on the cover of *National Geographic* magazine. Inside the magazine was a very heartwarming article about the bears who had saved a little girl and her father. The end of the article read, "Please don't shoot bears. They are not all as dangerous as they seem."

Several weeks later, the little girl and her father were released from the hospital, recovered and healthy. Betrees and Ben would have certainly welcomed that news, but they were already traveling to their honeymoon in the Northern Woods, far away from civilization.